Super Explorers

MW00902731

WEIRD CARS

Philip Hendriks

What is a Car?

A car is road vehicle that usually has four wheels, is powered by an engine and can carry a small number of people.

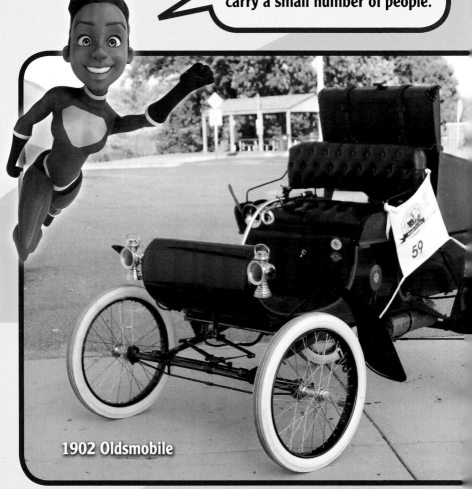

1902 Oldsmobile

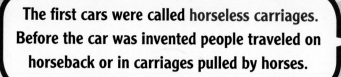

The first cars were called horseless carriages. Before the car was invented people traveled on horseback or in carriages pulled by horses.

Bennett Buggy

During the Depression of the 1930s, many car owners didn't have enough money to put gas in their cars. They would pull their cars with horses. These were called Bennett Buggies or Hoover Carts. A horseless carriage pulled by a horse...now that's weird!

Steam Cars

Stanley Steam Car

DS 7563

In the early 1900s, some cars used steam to power the engine. Water was heated in a boiler to make the steam. Hot steam pushed pistons that turned the crankshaft in the engine. Kerosene or gasoline was the fuel used to make the steam. Most of these cars are now only found in museums.

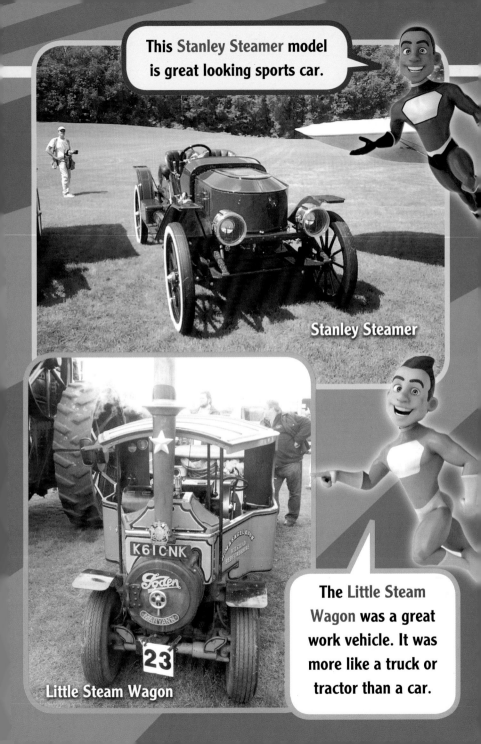

This **Stanley Steamer** model is great looking sports car.

Stanley Steamer

The **Little Steam Wagon** was a great work vehicle. It was more like a truck or tractor than a car.

Little Steam Wagon

Wheels

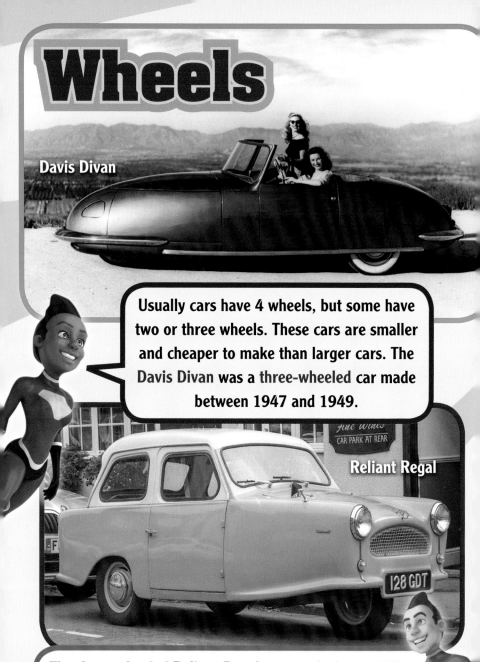

Davis Divan

Usually cars have 4 wheels, but some have two or three wheels. These cars are smaller and cheaper to make than larger cars. The Davis Divan was a three-wheeled car made between 1947 and 1949.

Reliant Regal

128 GDT

The three-wheeled Reliant Regal was made from 1953 to 1973 in England. It weighed only 445 kg (980 lb).

Lit C-1

The Lit C-1 is a two-wheeled **experimental** car. The company never did make a working unit. The Lomax 223 is a three-wheeled British kit car that you can build yourself.

Lomax 223

Tiny Cars

Peel Trident

Small cars have small engines and work great in cities with short winters. These cars can only carry one or two people.

Corbin Sparrow

The Corbin Sparrow is an electric, single-person car made for driving in cities.

Peel P50 A

FMP 62B

Some tiny cars have three wheels and others have four wheels. The Peel is the smallest car in the world.

The Smart Car can be found all over the world. It is a tiny car that can travel at highway speeds.

Smart Car

S·MB 1068

Low and High Cars

Cars can be low or high. The **ELVA MK7** is a car that is low to the ground. It has a roll bar for safety.

ELVA MK7

Donk Car

Some customized cars with tall wheels are called Donk cars. The car's suspension must be changed to make room for the tall wheels.

Wide and Narrow Cars

Cars can be wide or narrow. The Maserati MC12 is sports car that is as wide as a king-sized bed is long!

Maserati MC12

Messerschmidt K220

The Messerschmidt K220 is a weird car that is really narrow. It is only a little over one metre wide.

Wide Limo

Photo courtesy of www.jayohrberg.com

The Wide Limo is a novelty car that is very wide. How many people do you think can sit in the back seat?

Flying Cars

Some cars can fly or become airplanes.

Terrafugia

Terrafugia is a modern airplane that be converted to a car by folding its wings next to its fuselage.

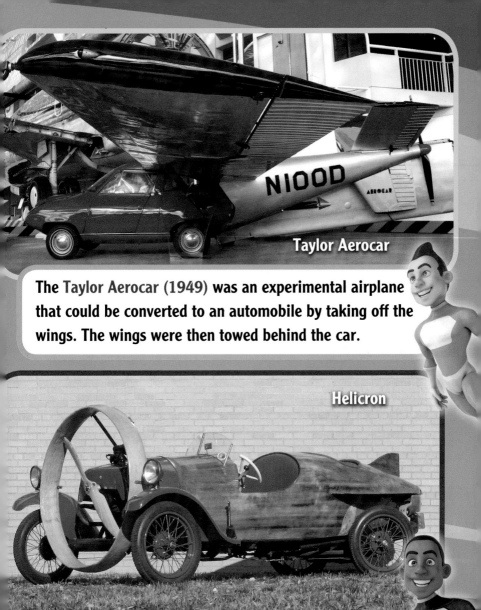

Taylor Aerocar

The Taylor Aerocar (1949) was an experimental airplane that could be converted to an automobile by taking off the wings. The wings were then towed behind the car.

Helicron

Air pushed by a large propeller moves the Helicron (1932) forward. Does this look like a safe car?

Amphibious Cars

Amphibious cars **can travel on land or on water.**

The **Amphicar** was made in Germany from 1961 to 1968. The engine drove the rear wheels, and in water, two propellers moved it along. It could go about 112 kph (70 mph) on land and 11 kph (7 mph) on the water.

Amphicar

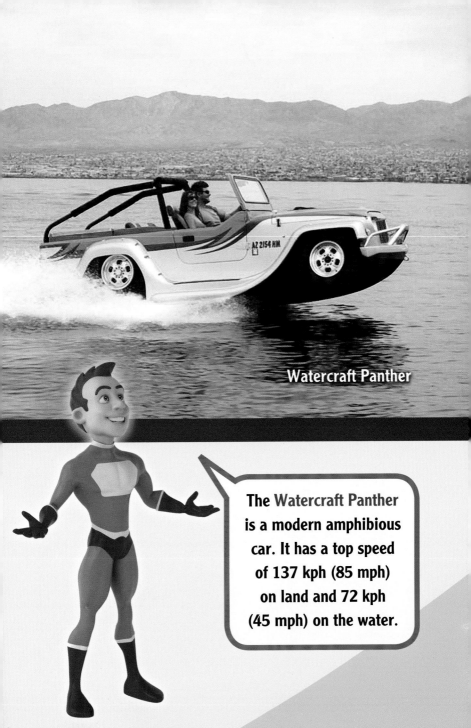

Watercraft Panther

The Watercraft Panther is a modern amphibious car. It has a top speed of 137 kph (85 mph) on land and 72 kph (45 mph) on the water.

Long Cars

Delorean Limo

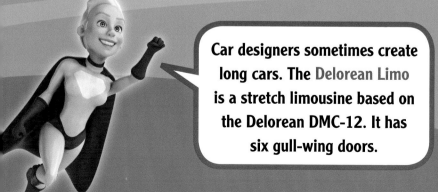

Car designers sometimes create long cars. The Delorean Limo is a stretch limousine based on the Delorean DMC-12. It has six gull-wing doors.

The American Dream is over 30 meters (100 feet) long. It has many creature comforts including a hot tub, a helicopter landing pad and 26 wheels.

American Dream

Photo courtesy of www.jayohrberg.com

The Cadillac 45 is 14 meters (45 feet) long. It has a chopped roof.

Cadillac 45

Photo courtesy of www.jayohrberg.com

Wooden Cars

Some cars have parts made of wood. The body of the Car of Wood is, of course, made of wood.

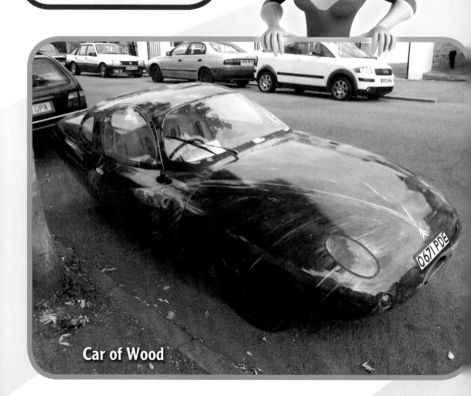

Car of Wood

Woodie

Morgan

Luxury Cars

Many luxury cars are long with beautiful interiors and powerful engines. Luxury cars are comfortable and stylish.

Maybach 6

Rolls Royce Phantom

Rolls Royce is a car company that make some of the world's most luxurious cars. These cars cost a lot to buy. They have excellent performance and comfort.

GHOST
BLACK BADGE

Rolls Royce Ghost

Slow Cars

Some cars can be slow. Most are meant for driving in the city.

The top speed of the electric Renault Twizy is 45 kph (28 mph).

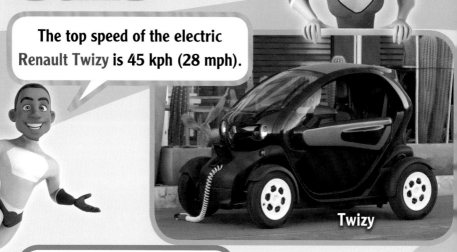

Twizy

The Aixam Coupe has a top speed of 93 kph (58 mph).

Aixam Coupe

Fast Cars

Supercars are the fastest road cars in the world.

Venom F5

The Hennessy Venom F5 has a top speed is 512 kph (318 mph).

The Bugatti Chiron's top speed is 417 kph (259 mph).

Chiron

Economical Cars

The Tata Nano can only be bought in India for $5200 CAD ($4000 USD).

Tata Nano

The Nissan Micra costs $9988 CAD ($7660 USD) to buy.

Micra

Sweptail

The Rolls Royce Sweptail is a custom-made car. It cost over $12 million USD!

Like the Sweptail, only one Maybach Exelero was ever made. It cost $8 million USD!

Exelero

Expensive Cars

Cars with Ads

Oscar Meyer Car

Businesses often use cars for advertising.

Hershey Kissmobile

Engine Cooling

The engine of the classic **Volkswagen Beetles** was air-cooled.

VW Beetle

The **Chevrolet Corvair** engine is air-cooled. Some people have used these engines in home-built airplanes!

Mixed-up Cars

A few car makers have made a vehicle that is part car and part truck.

Chevrolet El Camino

Subaru Brat

Chevrolet SSR

Ford Ranchero

Steering Wheels

Cars can have weird steering wheels.

The **Citroen DS** has a single spoke connecting the steering column to the steering box.

The **Austin Allegro Quartic** could be ordered with a squarish steering wheel.

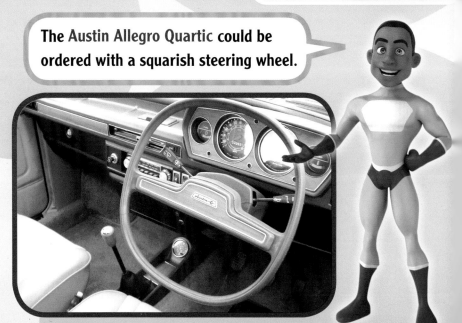

This Volkswagen has dual steering. It was used for driver education so the instructor could take control of the car if the student needed help.

The TRV Sagaris has a performance steering wheel designed for quick turning and handling.

Hot Rods

A hot rod is classic car (1930s to 1940s) that has been modified to have more power and change the way it looks.

Plymouth Prowler

The Plymouth Prowler has a small V6 engine. It is a modern version of a hot rod that was made from 1997 to 2002.

Hot Rod

People who build hot rods often want the cars to go quicker or make them look as if they go very fast.

Hot Rod with Flames

Shaped Cars

Some people build cars with interesting shapes.

Shoe Car

Dragon Car

Bathtub Car

These novelty cars are found in car collections or in museums. They can also be seen at special events like parades.

Barber Shop Car

Weird Car Doors

Designers sometimes build cars with different kinds of doors.

The Isetta has a door that opens from the front.

Isetta

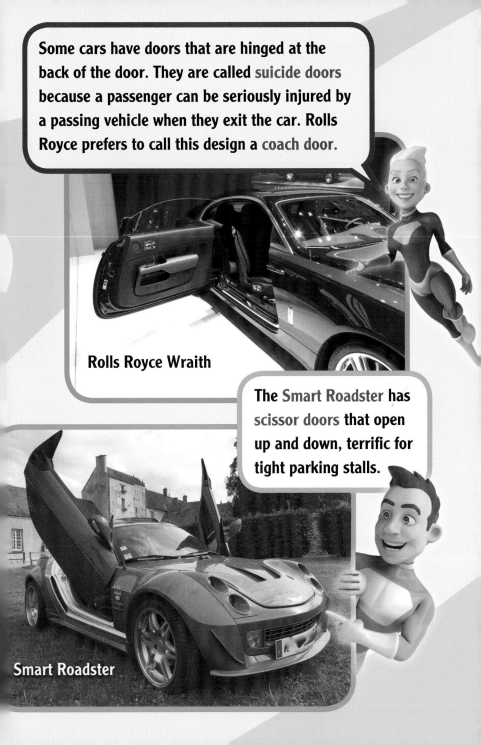

Some cars have doors that are hinged at the back of the door. They are called suicide doors because a passenger can be seriously injured by a passing vehicle when they exit the car. Rolls Royce prefers to call this design a coach door.

Rolls Royce Wraith

The Smart Roadster has scissor doors that open up and down, terrific for tight parking stalls.

Smart Roadster

More Weird Car Doors

Tesla Model X

More Than Four?

Four wheels are great, but some cars have more than four wheels. The Citroen Mille has ten wheels and was used to test tires made by Michelin.

Citroen Mille

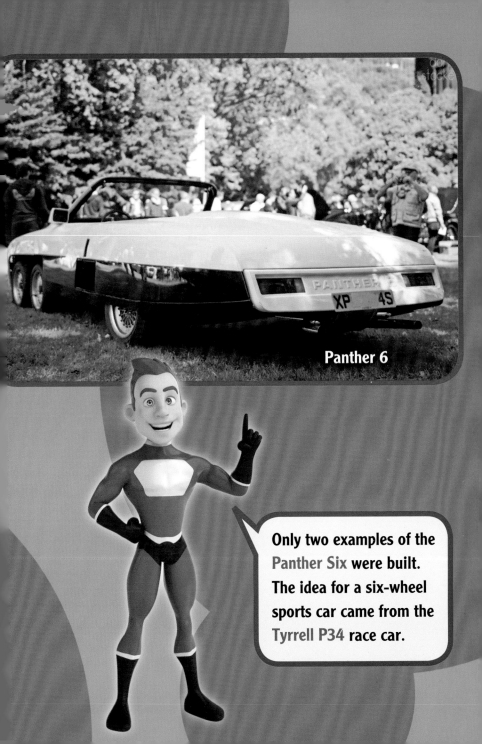

Panther 6

Only two examples of the Panther Six were built. The idea for a six-wheel sports car came from the Tyrrell P34 race car.

Convertibles and T-tops

Some cars have hard tops that can be moved off to make a convertible. Usually the top pulls back into the trunk.

Volvo C70

A **soft-top convertible** has a fabric roof that folds back like an accordion.

Fiat 500C

Corvette Stingray

You can remove panels from the roofs of these cars to make the roof open to the air. This type of roof is called a **T-Top** or a **T-Bar**.

Tall Cars

Some cars look weird because they are small and tall at the same time!

Nissan Cube

Where is the Engine?

Cars engines are mostly located in the front of the car under the hood. Some have been built with the engines in the middle or back of the car.

This Audi R8 has its engine in the middle of the car!

Audi R8

VW Beetle

The original Volkswagen Beetle had the engine in the back.

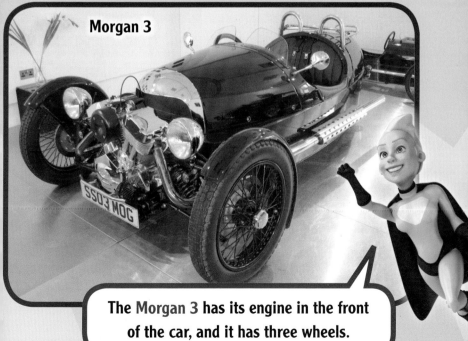

Morgan 3

The Morgan 3 has its engine in the front of the car, and it has three wheels.

Where do I sit?

Depending on the car, the driver and passengers can sit in different positions.

Messerschmitt KR220

The Messerschmitt KR220 has seats that are placed one behind the other, so it's like sitting in an airplane.

In the Johnson Presidential Rumble Seat Roadster passengers sat in the trunk!

Presidential Rumble Seat Roadster

McLaren F1

In the McClaren F1 the driver sits in the middle with passengers on either side.

Power!

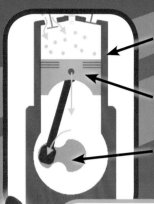

Cylinder

Piston

Crankshaft

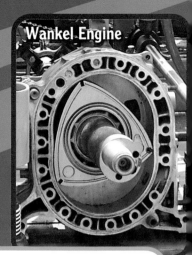

Wankel Engine

Most cars have engines that have pistons that go up and down to turn a crankshaft, making the car go forward. The Wankel engine has rotors that turn a shaft when fuel vapor is ignited in the combustion chamber that pushes the rotor.

The Mazda RX7 is powered by this type of rotary engine.

Mazda RX7

The **Chrysler Turbine Car,** made in 1963 and 1964, was powered by a jet engine. It drove like a regular car, but the engine could spin at 60,000 revolutions per minute (rpms). Most car engines spin about 1000 to 6000 rpms.

Chrysler Turbine Car

Supercharger

To get extra power, some cars have a supercharger on top of the engine. It gives more oxygen to the combustion chamber of the engine. The extra supply of oxygen increases the rate of combustion so the car can go faster.

High Tech Cars

Some car companies make hybrid cars that use gas engines *and* electric motors for power. The electricity is stored in batteries.

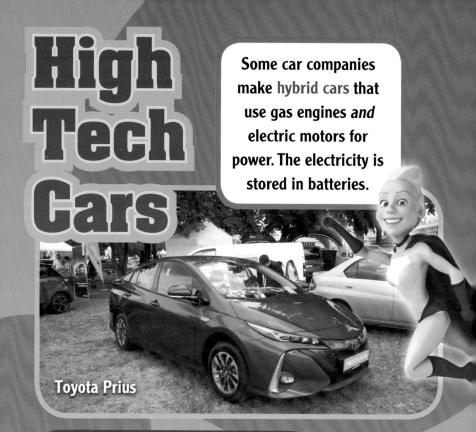

Toyota Prius

Some cars are entirely electric. The Tesla is a fast electric car that must be plugged in to charge its batteries.

Tesla Roadster

The Nissan Leaf is an electric car. Instead of filling up the tank with gas, you fill up the batteries with electricty!

Nissan Leaf

The Sunswift is a solar-powered race car made in Australia. The company hopes to make them available to the public soon.

Sunswift

Fun Cars

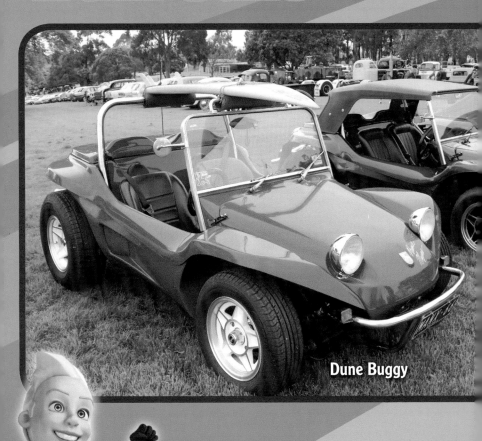

Dune Buggy

A Dune Buggy is a light vehicle that has excellent traction because it is short and has the weight of the engine over the rear wheels.

Some people build special cars to race on drag strips. This drag racing car races from a standing start as quickly as possible in a straight line down a 1/4-mile track. Usually pairs of cars race each other on a drag strip.

Pro Mod Drag Racing Car

A high-performance Pro Mod car can cover the distance in less than 6 seconds with a speed of over 400 kph (250 mph).

Racing Cars

Rally cars race down rural roads. The cars are timed from the start to the finish of a stage. A stage is about 50 kilometers (30 miles), and there are 15 to 30 stages. Each car has a driver and a navigator.

Rally Car

Most times, stock car races are held on oval tracks (0.4 kilometers to 4.25 kilometers, 1/4 mile to 2 2/3 miles long). Usually they are modified passengers cars. Some stock cars can go more than 320 kph (200 mph).

Movie Cars

There are cool cars used in movies and television shows.

The Batmobile is Batman's cool car that has armor and weapons to keep him safe.

Batmobile

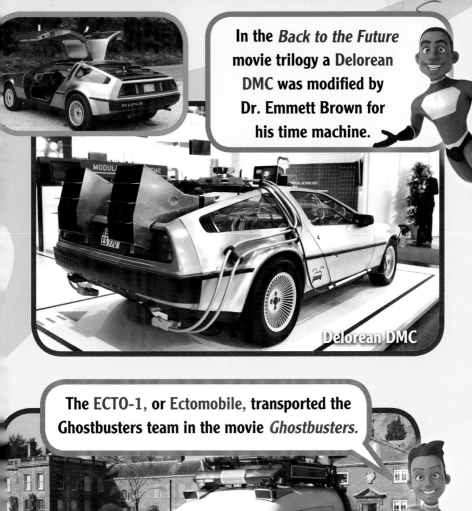

In the *Back to the Future* movie trilogy a Delorean DMC was modified by Dr. Emmett Brown for his time machine.

Delorean DMC

The ECTO-1, or Ectomobile, transported the Ghostbusters team in the movie *Ghostbusters*.

ECTO-1

The Publisher: Super Explorers is an imprint of Blue Bike Books

Library and Archives Canada Cataloguing in Publication

Hendriks, Philip, 1952–, author
  Weird cars / Philip Hendriks.

Issued in print and electronic formats.
ISBN 978-1-926700-94-6 (softcover).—ISBN 978-1-926700-95-3 (EPUB)

1. Automobiles—Miscellanea—Juvenile literature. 2. Experimental automobiles—Miscellanea—Juvenile literature. I. Title.

TL147.H46 2019	j629.222	C2018-905979-6
		C2018-905980-X

Front cover credit: From Wikimedia Commons, Kmr1985; from Getty Images, BethMyer.

Back cover credits: From Wikimedia Commons, Tom Harpel from Seattle, Washington, United States. From Flickr, Mike Weston. From Wikimedia Commons, Klaus Nahr

Photo Credits: From Wikimedia Commons: Agrestik 32a; Alexander Founder 26a; Alexander Migl 22, 23a; Alfvanbeem 7b, 47b; Andrew Bone 51a, 51b; Arnaud 25 34a; Bureau of Land Management 59b; c-g 38b; Ciar 15a; CZmarlin 55b; dave_7 21b; David Hunter 8a; David Villarreal Fernández 47a; Delta 51 24b; Dispvas2018 23b; Eliot from Las Vegas 53b; Frank Schwichtenberg 63b; Greg Gjerdingen 37b; GUMPERT Sportwagenmanufaktur GmbH 43; J. Lyon 54b; Jiří Sedláček 56a; John Robert Shepherd 34b; Jonathan Stonehouse 63c; Karrmann 55a; Kim H Yusuke~commonswiki 46; Klaus Nahr 44; Kmr1985 17; Leonid Mamchenkov 61a; Martin Cordes 53a; Matti Blume 25a; Michael Pereckas 14; Norbert Aepli 41a; Oldfarm 40; OSX 32b; Peustache 41b; Poudou99 62; PrinceArutha 57b; pschleut 59a; Ralf Roletschek 57a; Rama 24a; Robert Basic 9b; Royalbroil 61b; Sicnag 58; Simon Davison 27c; Tennen-Gas 48, 49a; The Quintessential DeLorean Website www.babbtechnology.com 63a; Tim Felce (Airwolfhound) 60; Tom Harpel from Seattle, Washington, United States 38a; Turnstange 42; Vauxford 6b; Xeper 49b. From Flickr: Andrew Basterfield 25b; Andrew Napier 54a; benjamin sTone 29a; Bill Abbott 31b; Brian Snelson 13a, 52; Charly W. Karl 27a, 27b; Chris Osborne 20; ClearFrost 50; Daniel Stocker 45; David Merrett 4; Don O'Brien 30b; Dru Bloomfield 10; Duncan Watson 7a; FotoSleuth 26b, 54c; Greg Gjerdingen 2, 33a, 36; Jacob Frey 4A 30a; Jared 16; Judy Schmidt 6a; Li Tsin Soon 28a; Mike Weston 8b; Nick Morozov 33b; Norm Hoekstra 28b; Peter Dutton 29b; Phillip Pessar 11; raneko 56b; Rex Gray 21a; Robert Sullivan 12; Stephen Pierzchala 5a; Steve 37a; Steven Tyler PJs 31a; The Car Spy 35b; Timitrius 5b, 9a; zombieite 18. Lane Motor Museum 15b; University of Saskatchewan 3; www.jayohrberg.com 13b, 19a, 19b, 39a, 39b; www.oldbug.com 35a.

Superhero Illustrations: julos/Thinkstock.

Produced with the assistance of the Government of Alberta.

We acknowledge the financial support of the Government of Canada.
Nous reconnaissons l'appui financier du gouvernement du Canada.

Funded by the Government of Canada
Financé par le gouvernement du Canada |